DREAMWORKS®

The PENGUINS
of MADAGASCAR

nickelodeon.

KING JULIEN'S
GUIDE
TO RULING
THE ZOO

by Michael Anthony Steele

Grosset & Dunlap
An Imprint of Penguin Group (USA) Inc

GROSSET & DUNLAP
Published by the Penguin Group
Penguin Group (USA) Inc., 375 Hudson Street,
New York, New York 10014, USA
Penguin Group (Canada), 90 Eglinton Avenue East, Suite 700, Toronto, Ontario M4P
2Y3, Canada (a division of Pearson Penguin Canada Inc.)
Penguin Books Ltd., 80 Strand, London WC2R 0RL, England
Penguin Group Ireland, 25 St. Stephen's Green, Dublin 2, Ireland
(a division of Penguin Books Ltd.)
Penguin Group (Australia), 250 Camberwell Road,
Camberwell, Victoria 3124, Australia (a division of Pearson Australia Group Pty. Ltd.)
Penguin Books India Pvt. Ltd., 11 Community Centre,
Panchsheel Park, New Delhi—110 017, India
Penguin Group (NZ), 67 Apollo Drive, Rosedale, Auckland 0632,
New Zealand (a division of Pearson New Zealand Ltd.)
Penguin Books (South Africa) (Pty.) Ltd., 24 Sturdee Avenue,
Rosebank, Johannesburg 2196, South Africa

Penguin Books Ltd., Registered Offices: 80 Strand, London WC2R 0RL, England

ISBN 978-0-448-45620-1   10 9 8 7 6 5 4 3 2 1

Hello there, book-reading person! It is I, your king. That's right—King Julien. But you can call me . . . King Julien.

Okay, settle down. Don't get so excited. I know it is quite an honor to be reading a book that I have been writing.

Are you settled down now? Really? For sure? Okay good.

Now, this book is all about how to rule the zoo like me. Of course, this is quite impossible for you because only *I* can be king. But who am I to take away your dreams? Oh, yes . . . I'm the king, that's who!

This is really going to be a treat for you, you know. This book contains all my kingly secrets. But most importantly, it is about my favorite subject—*me!* *M* to the *E*—me! And who better to write this book? Because no one loves me as much as *I* love me.

FIRST YOU NEED A KINGDOM!

You can't be a proper king or queen, silly person, unless you have a kingdom to rule. See, the word *king* is right there in the word *king*dom. That *proves* that a kingdom is super-important.

I suppose you could call your own room your kingdom . . . or queendom. Then you could rule over your stuffed animals, pets, little brothers or sisters . . .

 but it's not the same, really.

Now, as king of the New York Zoo *I* have quite a *large* kingdom. I often explore my kingdom on my many royal walkabouts.

This place is full of so many fantastical things. Did you know, for example, that there is free gum under all the benches?

Now I ask you this: What good is a king all alone in an empty kingdom? No good, I tell you! The royal kingdom must be filled with those who are to do my bidding!

WHICH BRINGS ME TO . . .

ZOO
MAP

ROYAL SUBJECTS

Come to think of it, I don't know why they are called "royal" subjects. *I* am the king and, therefore, I am the only one who should be "royal."

Nevertheless, my loyal royal subjects are good for all kinds of things—groveling, obeying, and combing the knots out of my tail.

Let me begin with my fellow lemurs. First there's Maurice, my chief adviser and primary pampering person. Then there's Mort. What can I say about Mort? He's annoying and a little pathetic. His only good quality is that he's a big fan of me.

My other subjects include my neighbors. There is Marlene, the otter. She's very nice but not so groveling enough, if you ask me.

There are also the panzees (or *chimpanzees* as Mason and Phil like to be called). I think they are a little *lowbrow* with all the poo-flinging, frankly.

And, of course, there are the silly Penguins. They are always doing the high-fiving and karate chopping all over the place. They aren't too annoying . . . except when they ignore my commands . . . don't take me seriously . . . and assault my kingly senses with their savage, fishy-smelling fishes. Yuck!

Oh no! This book has taken a wrong turn away from the fantastical subject of *me*! Let me get back on the track by telling you more about me.

OR AT LEAST ABOUT MY VERY FAVORITE KINGLY OBJECT . . .

THE KING'S CROWN

My crown is proof of my kingliness. It is nearly as awesome as I am!

Just look at it: It has a majestic palm frond chosen for its stately colors. They complement my luxurious fur and beautiful eyes, of course.

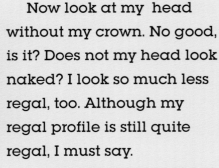

Now look at my head without my crown. No good, is it? Does not my head look naked? I look so much less regal, too. Although my regal profile is still quite regal, I must say.

I once traded my crown for a special helmet that the Penguins let me have (after I snuck in and took it from them). The helmet was perfect for me because it magically brought me things. This is something

every king should be having!

In the end I decided to go back to my old crown (mainly because the silly Penguins *ka-blewied* the helmet off of my head).

Besides, I have Maurice to bring me things. He even brought me my crown to cover my head's ka-blewied bald spot!

REMEMBER: EVERY KING NEEDS A ROYAL CROWN. WELL, THAT AND A ROYAL THRONE . . .

A king just *has* to have a throne! They are for sitting on and looking down upon people. You see, a good king knows how to make everyone else feel inferior. It's only proper.

My throne is very special. It has been passed down to me from generation to generation. It was hand carved from the wood of the largest baobab tree in all of Madagascar. And . . . it has a built-in seat warmer because my royal tushy gets freezy in the winter.

I think traditional thrones are best. Once I had Maurice build a

Supercomfy Pamper Time Floaty Throne. It was one of those things that sounded better on paper, let me tell you. I almost flew away, and I had to be rescued by . . . Mort! Can you be believing it?

MORT IS FOR PAMPERING—
NOT FOR RESCUING!

ROYAL PAMPERING

What good is being king if you cannot be properly pampered? That is what I am always saying. And look, I just said it again!

Lucky for me, as king, I am an expert at being pampered. I am skilled in the fine art of giving Maurice my blending order (for groovy smoothies).

I know just how to position myself for the royal sponge bath and the royal booty scratching. And I always know when I am about to sneeze. This way, I can have Mort hold my nose. Or if he's too late, he can act as the royal tissue. Don't worry. He loves it.

I know what you
may be asking yourself:
Is there not more to
life than just being
pampered all the time?
Well, like I always
say, there are no silly
questions . . . just silly
people asking them.

But, of course, there
is more to life than
being pampered
around the zoo!

A KING MUST ALSO BE
PAMPERED OUTSIDE
THE ZOO!

ROYAL TRAVEL

This is one king who likes to travel in style! Whether I'm driving the royal scooter or the royal adviser, I'm happy if I don't have to use my own muscles to get around.

For long trips, I ship myself super-platinum, premiere overnight express. This is how a king is to be rolling.

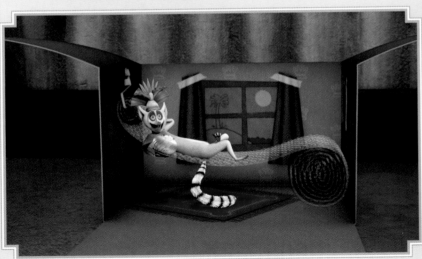

And when I reach my destination, I remember one very important kingly thing: Always give someone the honor of carrying the royal luggage. It is a courtesy, you see. Plus there is that thing again about me not using my own muscles.

Also, when a king arrives somewhere, he must be properly announced. Maurice is very good at this. One of my favorite announcements is "All hail, King Julien! Leader of the Lemurs and Lord of the Ringtails!" That one never gets old.

Remember: A good announcement is also a courtesy to the peoples. It helps remind them that I'm better than they are.

THIS IS HOW A KING SHOULD BE RULING!

KING JULIEN DAY

Nothing shows how important a king is than when that king (which, again, is me) has his very own holiday!

King Julien Day is the most bestest day of the year! It is a day where everybody loads the gifts upon me and pretty much does whatever I say. It's eight kinds of fun!

Then, at the end of the day, all of my subjects throw a party just for me! A me-esta, if you will.

I especially like the part where everyone bakes me a special cake. Because what is a party without a cake? Well, it's still a party, I suppose. But it feels as if something is missing— something cakey.

Don't forget the sharing of the sweets from the piñata's hiney! After all, I am a generous king.

HAPPY ME-DAY!

AN HEIR TO THE THRONE

Okay, it is true that I have lots of hairs all over my body. But that is not what I am talking about here. I'm talking about an *heir*. You know, someone to be the king later, after me (but not as good, obviously).

I AM KING JULIEN AND I APPROVE THIS FLASHBACK.

I once had my very own heir when Marlene found an egg left all by itself. I named it JJ (Julien Junior) and dreamed of raising it to be just like me—handsome,

brilliant, and, most of all, humble.

Unfortunately, it hatched and did not look at all like me. It was a duckling who would rather be more like a silly penguin than a regal ringtail!

That's okay. I know little JJ will be back someday. Because I have all the things a young person could admire—a blatant disregard for rules, down-with-it dance moves, and many material possessions.

WHICH BRINGS ME TO THE NEXT THING A KING NEEDS . . .

ROYAL TREASURE

This is very, very important: The king must have enough wealth and treasure to keep him 100 percent out of touch with the needs of his common subjects.

I'm talking *real* treasure. Not one of those "Friendship is the greatest treasure of all" deals. Because you can't trade friendship for, you know, the goods and services.

If you ask me, fruit is the best treasure of all! Fruit is sweet and tangy and juicy and sweet. Did I say *sweet* twice? It doesn't matter.

Fruit can be sweety-sweet. Except for grapes. I'm not completely on board with those.

The other great thing about fruit is that you can be throwing it at your loyal subjects!

HEE-HEE-HEE!

ABUSE OF POWER

What good is it to be king without being able to boss around the little people? Why am I asking you? You are a little person. *I* am the king!

Sometimes, as king, I like to "borrow" things. Like when I borrow the Penguins' delicious food for my stomach. Or when I borrow their TV. Or when I borrow their toothbrushes to scrub my hard-to-reach nether regions. This ruffles the Penguins' feathery parts, but I don't care. This is what is great about being king!

Also, as king, I get to make everyone do the work while I watch with anticipation. This, too, is one of the perks.

I am not a bad king, though. I always do the right thing . . . eventually . . . when there's no

other choice. But I will never apologize! My policy on apologizing is clear: It is for the weak and wrong. In fact, if anyone demands an apology from me, I demand an apology for *them* demanding an apology!

I HAVE SEVERAL RULES LIKE THAT . . .

ROYAL DECREES

A king must be constantly making up rules to keep his subjects in line.

These are called decrees, and I'm famous for them. A couple of my decrees are "Nobody tells the king 'I told you so!'" and "The king, which is me, shall never lift heavy things!"

However, one of my best decrees is "From this moment (which is happening now) and on, anyone who touches the king's feet (which are mine) will

be punished most savagely. They will be banished forever or for eternity . . . I'm flexible."

Mort was not so very good at keeping away from the royal feet, so I banished him a little.

Don't worry. I let him come back eventually. As king, I can break my own rules anytime I want. Again, this is one of the perks.

Now always remember: A king must keep coming up with these important rules, no matter how silly they seem.

LUCKILY, I'M THE BEST AT THAT. IN FACT, BEING KING MEANS YOU HAVE TO BE THE BEST AT ALMOST EVERYTHING!

BE THE BEST

Being the king means never having to say you're sorry. And it also means never having to say "Congratulations on winning that thing!" because *I* am the one who is always winning because *I* am the best.

The silly Penguins think they are the best with all their secret missions and code-talky things. But the king is always the best; that is just the way it is. I even beat the Penguins many times at their own capture the flag game. It was quite fun and satisfying.

As the best, I deserve many, many trophies. Trophies not only *show* everyone that I am the best, but I can also see my reflection in their shiny goodness. It's a win-win situation!

I'm the best at dancing, the best at being pampered, and the best at roller-skating. And one time, it was I (not the Penguins) who scared away the evil spirits from Marlene's habitat. I did it with my special spirit-scaring dance skills. Did I mention that I was the best at dancing, too?

Of course, these were regular, plain-evil spirits.

NOT THE FAMOUS . . . SKY SPIRITS!

KEEP THE SKY SPIRITS HAPPY

As king, I am so special, the sky spirits send me signs—because I am king. Some people say (and I won't name the names of the Penguins or the Chimps) that believing in the sky spirits is nothing

but superstitions. To that I say . . . *yes!* These stitions *are* super! They are the sky spirits!

Unfortunately, I don't always please the sky spirits. There was the time when they trapped Maurice inside a magic thingy which they dropped into my habitat. The Penguins called it a "camera." But I know it was a

magic king thing the sky spirits gifted to me. It didn't matter, though. Maurice was gone!

I begged and pleaded for them to return my big-bootied buddy. Luckily, the sky spirits took pity on me and released Maurice. He was just in time for my four o'clock pampering!

The Penguins tried to tell me that Maurice had simply run away for a little bit. But the Penguins don't know the sky spirits like I do! Silly Penguins.

Just as the sky spirits watch over me, I like to pass along that good juju by watching over my own peoples.

A GOOD KING ALWAYS REMEMBERS THIS.

SPY ON YOUR SUBJECTS

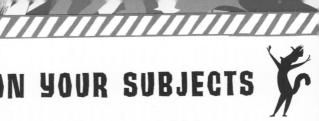

A king must constantly keep a watchful eye on his kingdom—especially his subjects. Not only are my subjects all the time getting into trouble (which sometimes I cause), but also they are more fun to watch than any show on TV! They are the realest of the reality shows!

My subjects are a slippery bunch— especially the slippy-sliding Penguins. One time I had to keep a very close watch on them. They were trying to get more stinky fish that are all the time smelling up the royal nose. *Pee-yew!*

Another time, I had to sneak around and taunt Skipper. He wouldn't accept my challenge to beat him at his capture the flag game! The taunting was more just for fun, though.

I must tell you, I am the sneakiest of the sneakies. I can

be watching from almost anywhere at any time. I could be sneaking up behind you right now! Just kidding! Made you look, you silly person.

But seriously, being a sneaky king isn't just always for my own entertainment purposes. One thing a king must remember is that he can't trust anybody.

OKAY, JUST BECAUSE I'M PARANOID DOESN'T MEAN THAT EVERYONE ISN'T *REALLY* OUT TO GET ME!

WATCH OUT FOR USURPERS

A usurper isn't someone who steals a nice fruit smoothie. I didn't say a "you-*slurper*." A *usurper* is someone who wants to steal my throne. This happens when *they* are wanting to be king!

Everyone is jealous of the king, you see. Perhaps it is my rugged, good looks. Or maybe it is my boogie-rific dance moves. Whatever it is, I have to be very careful of being king-napped at any moment (or at least somewhat inconvenienced).

I never know from where the attack will come. It could be from the silly Penguins; the red-bootied baboons; or even Alice, the strange,

shorty-pants lady who thinks she runs the zoo. She doesn't know who is *really* in charge, let me tell you. Or if she does, she has a funny way of showing it.

Okay, I get it. Everybody just wants to be me (or at least be *close* to me).

LUCKY FOR THEM, THERE IS ENOUGH OF ME TO GO AROUND!

KINGLY SOUVENIRS!

As king, I have become somewhat of a celebrity.
Who am I kidding? I am a *lot*-what of a celebrity! And

everyone knows that the
most important part of being
a celebrity is having plenty
of me-shaped products! This
is also something very nice
to do for the peoples, you
see. This way they can buy a
product and then bask in my
kingliness wherever they go!

Take this me-shaped
drink cup. It is awesome, just
like me! You can even sip a refreshing beverage from

its head. Not even
my *real* head does
that! Just don't slurp
too hard or you will
end up with a flat,
squishy thing that
doesn't look at all
like me. And nobody
wants that.

It should be said (which is why I am saying it) that a king should inspect every piece of kingly product. Take my King Julien doll. The peoples who made it got the crown all wrong. And my noble nose was looking way too big. There was no quality controlling, I tell you!

On the other hand, the Mort doll came out just perfectly. A little too perfectly, if you are asking me. Which brings me to the other rule about merchandising: Always stink up the competition in the skunk pen.

PROBLEM SOLVED!

BE A PROBLEM SOLVER

One of my royal duties (and, no, I don't mean that kind of *doody*) is to step in and solve my subjects' petty disputes. By the powers infested in me, I have the answer to *all* of their problems. I'm often asked to take control of a crisis. Even when I'm not asked, I sometimes do it, anyway.

After hearing my subjects' baby squeals for help, *I* (which is me, the king) must use my superior big brain and plan to come up with a carefully-planned plan.

Sometimes the plan is to outwit someone with my outwittiest of wits—like my brilliant strategy of running away in terror when Marlene had the cooties. Then there was the time Mort became trapped inside the popcorn cart. I used my royal brain to make the

wisest of decisions.
I made everyone
work together to
free . . . the delicious
poppity corn! After
all, why should
Mort keep it all
to himself?

UH! ALL OF THIS KINGLY THINKING
MAKES ME VERY TIRED.

ROYAL RESTING

You will find out when you are king (which you won't be, because only *I* am king) that after all of your kingly duties (again, that is not *that* kind of *doody*), you will need plenty of resting time.

I find that I need a good eight hours of sleep at night so I can be at the peak of bossiness during the day.

And don't forget the royal naps! I know that *I* never do!
There is my morning post-pampering nap. My
pre-lunch nap. My post-lunch nap. My four o'clock
combination high tea and siesta. And then there's my
early evening pre-sleep nap. This is so I can be quite
rested for the royal sleep.

Between the napping and the pampering and the
ordering of peoples around, a king's day is quite full.

I STILL LIKE TO SQUEEZE
IN A LITTLE ME TIME.

HAVE SOME ROYAL HOBBIES

A king cannot live on sleep, feasting, and pampering alone. Well, actually, I do. But I also make time for my many hobbies. You have to prioritize.

There are many things that help break up the monotony of ordering everyone around all the time.

I like to dance for the silly humans so they throw the delicious poppity corn at us. Sometimes I bounce in my bounce house until

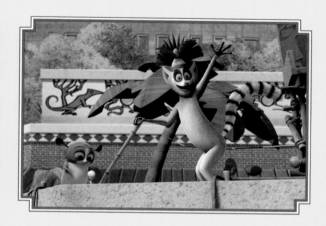

my tummy tingles.

I even roller-skate around the zoo. And I like to hit some golf balls into the penguin habitat. They are the perfect distance away to help me work on my game, you know.

And don't forget a little light meditation.

I FIND THAT THIS HELPS ME UNWIND FROM ONE OF MY MANY ROYAL ADVENTURES.

LEADING ADVENTURES

The Penguins are all the time going on adventures. Skipper likes to say he leads these so-called "missions," but I think I should be leading, don't you? After all, who

is better in the leadership department than a king? Unless, of course, that leader happens to be up against a giant, mutant rat. Then I think Skipper should definitely be in charge.

On one adventure, I was king-napped by the silly Penguins' even sillier archenemy, the evil Dr. Blowhole. He is one crazy dolphin, yet his skin is surprisingly pleasant to the touch. But don't worry. I talked him into

letting me go. Then we joined forces to defeat the Penguins! Ha-ha!

That dastardly dolphin didn't know that I was really . . . a double agent. I was a good-guy

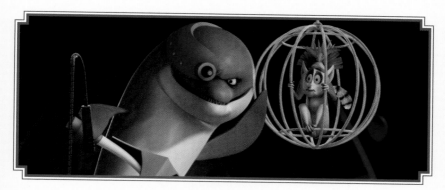

spy! I saved the Penguins and Dr. Blowhole ran away like a little scaredy-baby. This was one of my better triumphs, really.

My only regret is that I didn't have a cool spy car that shot things out of the headlights. No one would expect that.

The excitement of the adventures always gives me the tinglies! So I have Maurice scratch me until the tinglies go away. Maurice is not as good as the Penguins in the adventure department. He doesn't have any karate-chop commando skills. He excels more in smoothie-blending and administration.

But I don't let Maurice's shortcomings bring me down!

WAIT, THERE'S MORE!

A KINGLY ATTITUDE

That's right! This is probably the most important part about being king. You see, I am brimming with confidence. There is nothing I cannot do. Except kiss

up to my own hiney, and that is what Mort is for.

Do you think this kingly attitude comes naturally? Well, yes, for me it does. But for anybody else, it would take years of practice to become this noble, dignified, and superior. Plus, I like to mix in a little kooky. That way I get to use the

crazy eyes once in a while.

Wait a minute. Did I say a kingly attitude was the most important part of being a king? Well, I didn't say that, because if I did, I would have been wrong. And I am never wrong!

Actually, the most important thing about being a king is . . .

NOW PAY ATTENTION . . .
HERE IT COMES . . .

KINGLY DANCE MOVES

That's right! You didn't see that one coming toward you, did you?

This is one king who knows how to get down and boogie. I'm boogie-riffic! I am bringing it to the street and keeping it realistic!

You should see what this kingly booty can do! I can do the mambo, the moonwalk, the Egyptian, the electric noodle, the robot . . . I am the limbo king! I am even the crazy conga king!

Maurice turns on our boomy box, and we dance

all night long. We lemurs go all night because the baboons once shook their shiny, red bottoms eighteen hours straight, and I will not be out-partied!

If you want to be king, you must really learn to shake your booty. Just take the music inside of you, swish it around, and spit it out through your tail.

REMEMBER, A STILL BOOTY IS A SAD BOOTY!

So there you are having it! That is everything you need to know on how to be king and the ruling of the zoo. Why did I tell you all of these secrets? Because *you* can never be king, silly book-reading person. Only *I* can be king! You really should be knowing this already. I said it right there on the first page.

However, if you are truly more interested in my kingliness, come to the zoo and apply for one of my intern, groveling positions. It will take many years of training. But if you work hard and pay attention to all of my decrees, then maybe you can someday scratch the royal hiney. It is quite an honor, really.

SINCERELY, YOURS TRULY,

KING JULIEN